THE BOLDS'

Great Adventure

by
Julian Clary

Illustrated by
David Roberts

Andersen Press · London

First published in 2018 by Andersen Press Limited
20 Vauxhall Bridge Road London SW1V 2SA
www.andersenpress.co.uk

2 4 6 8 10 9 7 5 3 1

British Library Cataloguing in Publication Data available.

ISBN 978 1 78344 629 2

Printed and bound in Great Britain by
Clays Limited, Bungay, Suffolk, NR35 1ED

Chapter

Parents are a funny lot, aren't they? Full of surprises! My mother once met me from school wearing a pair of knickers on her head. She said it was World Knickers Day, but of course there's no such thing. She was just being silly.

And my father encouraged me to read and write, but then seemed less keen when I wrote on my bedroom wall

with felt-tip pen. Make your mind up!

But it is true, I suppose, that parents know things we don't. They're bound to because they're so old. And it can be worth listening to them sometimes.

Occasionally parents say something interesting, if only by the law of averages. And parents know things too: what you're having for tea, whether you've washed your hands or not, where your birthday presents are hidden. And what the family secrets are . . .

This is a story about a very surprising family secret told to Betty and Bobby Bold by their parents, the evening before their first day at school. It is a story that is hard to believe. But I assure you it is true. I mean, if I was going to make something up, it wouldn't be as incredible as the tale I'm about to tell you, trust me!

Betty and Bobby are twins and they live with their parents in a lovely semi-detached house in Teddington. On this particular night they were ready for bed – their teeth cleaned (they both have very large, pointy teeth) and their ears brushed (they both have very hairy ears).

They were waiting for their mother to tuck them in and their father to tell them a goodnight joke – Mr Bold loves jokes and has a job writing them for Christmas crackers.

But when they came into the room, their parents were looking very serious. Which was most unusual, because Mr and Mrs Bold are the most fun parents you could ever meet – always laughing and telling jokes.

'What's wrong, Dad?' asked Betty.

'You look worried,' said Bobby.

Mr Bold sat himself on the end of Betty's bed and coughed a couple of times. His wife put her hand on his shoulder and gave it a little squeeze. 'Come on, dear,' she said. 'We've got to tell them.'

'Tell us what?' asked Betty.

'Tell you who you really are,' said her mother.

The twins didn't understand and looked at each other in confusion.

'Have you ever noticed that you're different from other people?' asked Mr Bold.

'Well, I suppose our teeth are bigger than others',' suggested Bobby.

'And we're a bit hairier than other children,' said Betty.

'And we can't stop laughing,' said Bobby, and his shoulders started to shake as the giggles erupted from inside him.

'Precisely,' said his mother. 'But there's a reason for all that, my dear. A very unusual, rather special reason.'

'Yes,' agreed her husband. 'You see it's so unusual, we've been keeping it a secret. But now you're going to school, we think it's time to tell you.'

'Tell us what?' asked Bobby.

Mrs Bold opened her mouth to speak but no words came out.

'What your mother is trying to tell you is that the reason we're not like other people is because we're not really people at all,' said Mr Bold.

'What?!' Bobby howled with laughter. 'What are we then? A computer game? Aliens?'

'Oh no,' said his mother. 'Something much more unusual than that.'

'We're hyenas,' stated Mr Bold. 'Hyenas from Africa living in disguise as humans. And so far no one has discovered our secret. And that's the way we want it to stay.'

As family secrets go, this is quite a shocker, don't you think? The sort of thing that would keep you or I awake all night, wondering about it. But Bobby scratched his hairy ears and Betty ran her tongue across her pointy teeth, and they both began to consider whether it could really be true.

'Africa?' said Bobby.

'Hyenas?' said Betty.

The twins looked at each other and started to laugh.

'This is the funniest joke you've ever told us, Dad.'

'It's not a joke, son. Far from it. For once in my life, I'm being serious.'

'We don't believe you,' said Betty.

'Can you prove it?' demanded Bobby.

Mrs Bold looked at her husband, who nodded. 'Yes children, I can,' she said. 'Look inside your pyjama bottoms and tell me what you can see there, apart from your legs and, er, private parts.'

The twins did as their mother suggested.

'Round the back,' said their father, helpfully.

'This?' asked Betty, pulling out a long, furry tail.

'I've got one too,' said Bobby, producing his own tail. 'Don't all children have these?'

'No dear, they don't,' said Mrs Bold. 'Now show them the photo, Fred.'

So Mr Bold produced a book called *Animals of Africa*, and opened it at a particular page.

'Here,' he said. 'Take a look. This is a

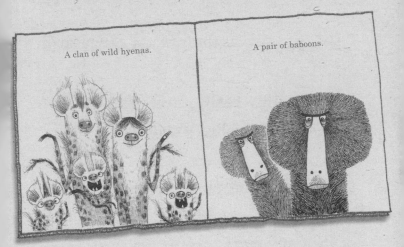

A clan of wild hyenas.

A pair of baboons.

family of wild hyenas. Look at the cubs. Remind you of anyone?'

The twins' eyes widened in wonderment.

'Wow!' said Bobby.

'They're just like *us*!' said Betty. 'And they've got tails, just like us!'

'Human beings most certainly don't have tails,' pointed out Mrs Bold.

'Now do you believe us?' asked Mr Bold.

'We really, really are wild African hyenas?' said Bobby. 'Brilliant!'

Mrs Bold held up a paw sternly. 'No, Bobby. Hyenas, yes. Wild hyenas, definitely not. Not any more.'

'But how did we get here?' asked Betty, frowning.

'We've got a lot to tell you, children,' answered her mother. 'Settle down and listen carefully. This is our Bolds' Family Secret.'

Chapter

2

'Your mother and I haven't always been called Amelia and Fred Bold,' began the twins' father. 'We used to be Sue and Spot when we were hyenas living in Africa. Every day we scavenged for meat, rubbed our bottoms on plants and laughed along with the rest of our clan.

'We lived very near a safari camp and the human beings there were always leaving scraps of food around. So *most* nights we would creep in, on the lookout for something to eat, and then listen to the stories they told each other round the campfire. Well, we animals are a lot more intelligent than people realise and it wasn't long before your mother and I learned to speak human – in particular English, as many of the visitors to the camp were from England.'

'One evening your father and I were going for a stroll when we came across a large pond,'

continued Mrs Bold. 'Then we found some human clothes discarded on the side. Guess what? Some foolish humans had gone for a swim in the pond and been **eaten** by a crocodile.'

Betty gasped in shock.

'I know, dear,' said Mrs Bold, giving Betty a comforting stroke. 'But these things happen in the wild. Survival of the fittest and the smartest. It's dog eat dog. Or croc eat human, in this particular case. They wouldn't have suffered. It would all have been over in a snap.'

'Well, your mother and I had a rummage around,' Mr Bold said, 'and soon found amongst the clothes two passports, aeroplane tickets to England, a driving licence, and house keys to 41 Fairfield Road.'

'That's our house!' exclaimed Bobby.

'That's right,' said his father. 'But at

the time it belonged to Mr and Mrs Bold.'

'But you're Mr and Mrs Bold.'

'Well, we are now, but at that time we were Sue and Spot the hyenas.'

'Were Mr and Mrs Bold the people eaten by the crocodile?' asked Betty.

'Yes, they were,' said Mr Bold (who wasn't Mr Bold at the time of the crocodile incident, of course, but Spot.)

'Well I suddenly had the boldest idea ever,' said Mrs Bold (or should I say Sue the hyena? Try to keep up.) 'I asked whether your father could walk on his hind legs and without hesitation he jumped up to show me. I then convinced him to try on the clothes with me and they fitted us beautifully. So, tucking in our tails and hiding our hairy ears beneath hats, we decided to pretend to be Mr and Mrs Bold and leave the safari park for an adventure and new life in England.'

'Are you for real?' asked Betty.

'I promise you,' said her father.

'It was terribly hot out there, dear,' explained her mother. 'Played havoc with my mange. So that evening your father and I walked into the safari camp on our hind legs.

'"Good evening, Mr and Mrs Bold," said the man on reception. "Have you had a nice afternoon?"

'"Yes thank you," I said. "We've just been for a swim in the watering hole."

'"Oh, you must be very careful," said the man. "There are lots of crocodiles living there. You could have been eaten alive."

'Your father and I couldn't help it, we started to laugh. Well it's what hyenas are famous for.

'"Are you all right?" asked the man on reception.

'"Oh yes, fine. Sorry, just dead tired."

'"Well, here are the keys to your room. Why don't you get some sleep? The bus to take you to the airport will be here in the morning at five o'clock sharp. Good night."

'"Good night," we said. He gave us the keys and we stared at them – they had a small key ring attached with some funny squiggles over it.

'"What are these for?" asked your father. We didn't know humans locked their doors. Whoever heard of such a thing? Hyenas might not be the most popular creatures in the animal kingdom, but we certainly never go into each other's burrows to steal things.

'"They're the keys to your room, of course," said the receptionist. "Number 531, at the end of the corridor."

'"Of course," I said. "My husband is being very silly!"

'We tottered down the corridor to our room and shut the door behind us. It was the beginning of our exciting adventure – and there was no going back now. But of course we had an awful lot to learn!'

Mr and Mrs Bold began to laugh at the memory.

'Your father had a drink out of the toilet!'

'Your mother did a poo in the shower!'

'We slept in the mini bar!'

'We drank the bubble bath!'

'We ate the wooden fruit bowl!'

'And the pillows!'

'We were laughing so much, Reception phoned, asking us to keep the noise down. But of course we'd never heard a phone ring before. When it started your father thought it was some sort of rodent and bit it. Then we heard an irritable voice say, "Mr Bold? Could we ask you to please make a little less noise?" It's a wonder we weren't rumbled.'

'The state we left the honeymoon suite in! Terrible, really. Goodness knows what they must have thought.' Fred and Amelia shook their heads at the memory of it all.

But then Mrs Bold continued the story. 'We'd better crack on, Fred. So much more to explain to the children.'

'Yes, indeed,' agreed Mr Bold. 'So, somehow we managed to pack our cases and get onto the bus to the airport.

Which is where it happened for the first time . . .'

'What did?' asked Betty.

'Your father heard his first joke. From the driver.'

'What was it?' asked Bobby.

Why did the bus stop?

Because it saw the zebra crossing!

'I thought it was the funniest thing I'd ever heard, and I laughed hysterically for so long, people began to stare.'

'Of course we didn't want that, so I managed to calm your father down eventually by putting his head between his knees. And that was the first, and really the most important, lesson we learned.'

'Don't draw attention to yourself!'

'A very important lesson, children. If people start to scrutinise you too closely, they might notice things about you that will get them thinking. And when human beings think too much, it always leads to trouble.'

'Got it,' said Bobby and Betty together.

'So what happened next?' asked Betty, wide awake and eager to hear the next bit of the Bolds' adventure.

'Well, it all got a bit tricky, I can tell you,' said her mother.

'Our adventure was almost over before it began,' agreed Mr Bold, shuddering as he remembered what happened.

'Oh no!' said Bobby, pulling the duvet up to his furry chin.

'The airport,' said Mrs Bold darkly. 'A strange and dangerous place for a hyena. For lots of reasons.'

'Tell us, tell us!' cried the twins.

'Very well, we will,' said Mr Bold.

He told the twins to snuggle down and get comfortable under their duvets. Mr and Mrs Bold perched on the ends of their beds. It was going to be the longest and most remarkable bedtime story the twins had ever heard.

Chapter

And so Mr and Mrs Bold continued to tell their children the incredible story. It's a shocking tale and goes like this . . .

When Mr and Mrs Bold arrived at Kilimanjaro Airport, they were feeling nervous and a little queasy. They had never been on a bus before and the bumpy ride gave them both a headache. The sight of the big concrete building, with its high ceilings and lots of official security people wandering around, did little to calm their nerves. Unsure what to do, they just followed their fellow travellers off the bus, collected their suitcases and joined the queue for what was called 'Baggage Check In'. Whatever that meant.

'Oh dear, Fred,' said Amelia. 'We're never going to get away with this. Whatever were we thinking?'

'Stay calm,' said Fred. 'As long as we keep our hats on and our heads down, we should be fine. We'll just do what everyone else does.'

Suddenly they were at the front of the queue.

'Tickets and passports,' said the man behind the counter.

'Oh, er, yes, of course,' said a flustered Amelia, fishing into her handbag and pulling out a used tissue and a packet of mints. 'Here you are!'

'No, madam,' said the man crossly. 'Tickets and passports, I said.'

'Oh, I'm a silly old hyena, er, I mean Sheila, I mean Amelia, er, woman, um, human being. I'm not a hyena. Never have been!'

'Excuse my wife,' said Fred, reaching into the handbag and passing the man the proper documents. 'She's a nervous flyer.'

The man rolled his eyes and typed some details into his computer.

'Did you pack these bags yourself?'

'Oh yes,' nodded Fred. 'First time for everything.'

'Window or aisle?'

'You'll what?'

'Where would you like to sit?'

'On the plane, please.'

The man sighed and handed them back their tickets and passports. 'Make your way to Passport Control. Just over there.'

'So far so good,' said Fred to Amelia as they joined the next queue.

'This is the tricky bit,' said his wife. 'From the look of it, they seem to be comparing people's faces to the photos in their passports. Are we sure we want to do this? Leave our old life behind for ever? Supposing we don't like living in England?'

'Oh, we will, I'm sure,' reassured Fred,

taking hold of his wife's paw. 'A new life, Sue – I mean Amelia. A big new adventure!'

Just then their conversation was interrupted by a low growl. A security guard was leading a sniffer dog along the queue and it had stopped next to the Bolds and was sniffing at them with great interest.

'Ooh-er!' said Fred. 'Can I help you?'

'You're a pair of hyenas!' declared the sniffer dog. Fortunately he said this in animal language, so his handler couldn't understand. 'What are you up to?'

'Oh, we're off to England. Don't give the game away old boy, please!'

'No worries,' said the dog. 'But go for the passport control cubicle on the left . . . the lady there will understand,' said the dog, giving the two nervous hyenas a wink.

'Thank you,' said Mrs Bold.

'I'd better move on before my handler gets suspicious. Good luck!' he said cheerily, and began to sniff the next people in the queue.

When they got to the recommended cubicle, Mr and Mrs Bold realised why it was a good idea: sitting in the cubicle, wearing a smart uniform, earrings and lipstick, was an ostrich. Can you believe it? The Bolds recognised her at once. It was Dolores. She used to be seen racing across Serengeti National Park near their hyena burrow, until she suddenly disappeared about six months ago. Everyone assumed she'd been eaten by a lion, but now it seemed that she'd had a similar idea to the Bolds and decided to try living as a human being. Mr Bold gave the ostrich a knowing smile as he handed over the passports.

'Here they are,'

said Fred. 'Without feather ado . . .'

The ostrich's eyes widened in surprise. 'Spot and Sue, I do declare!'

'Er, Fred and Amelia, you mean,' said Fred, glancing over his shoulder. 'As it says in our passports. Look.'

The ostrich cleared her throat. 'Everything seems to be in order. Have you enjoyed your holiday?'

'It was very pheasant, I mean pleasant.' Fred lowered his voice. 'Nice to see you, Dolores. You're working here now, then? Since wren? Er, when?'

'I had to get away,' said Dolores quietly. 'Life as an ostrich was fowl.' She handed back the passports. 'Have a good flight, and good luck!'

'Thanks – and same to you!' smiled the Bolds, and they were on their way.

There was almost a disaster when Fred thought he was supposed to sit on the conveyor belt to go through the security X-ray machine, but Amelia managed to stop him before he climbed on.

'I think it's just for hand luggage, dear,' she cautioned. 'Your tail would show up on the X-ray machine, and I don't think that would be helpful.'

So before they knew it, Mr and Mrs Bold were sitting on the plane as it taxied along the runway for takeoff. They had seen planes flying high above them when they were living on the Serengeti, but they could never quite imagine being on one and travelling through the sky themselves. Now they were about to find out what it was like.

But first there was the safety demonstration. The Bolds listened attentively until the flight attendant placed the oxygen mask over her face. To two hyenas the mask looked very like a snout, and reminded them of something they'd seen before.

'It's a warthog!' declared Fred.

'Oh my goodness, **exactly** like one!' said Amelia. And then the Bolds began to hoot and cackle, and once they started, they were unable to stop. The man sitting in front of the Bolds had heard the remark, and had a chuckle himself.

'Hey,' he said, looking through the gap in the seats.

What do you give a sick hog?

Oinkment!

'Ah, ha ha ha!' laughed Mr Bold.

Pleased his joke had gone down so well,
the man tried another.

This was too much for the Bolds, and had it not been for their seat belts, they'd have been rolling in the aisles. They were laughing so loudly, the flight attendant glared at them.

'Please pay attention,' she said sternly. 'The demonstration is for your own safety.'

Mrs Bold elbowed her husband in the ribs.

'We do apologise,' she said, trying her best to keep a straight face. 'But we just heard a crackling joke.'

Fred and Amelia found the takeoff very exhilarating, and whooped with excitement. Then there was the thrill of the refreshments trolley coming round.

The Bolds tried a fizzy drink for the first time and the feeling of the bubbles in their mouths made them laugh again. But it had been a long morning, full of new experiences, and tiredness soon swept over them. Being hyenas, they didn't sleep sitting up in their seats, but curled into a ball, like a dog in front of the fire. People passing down the aisle thought this rather strange. But not strange enough to think the Bolds were anything other than rather eccentric human beings.

As they drifted off to sleep, both Fred and Amelia were wondering what the future had in store for them and whether they would really be able to carry off their new identities. The Serengeti was lovely, but they were an adventurous young couple and they wanted to experience new things. There was a big, wonderful world out there and they wanted to explore it all. Seeing Dolores working as a passport inspector at the airport had reassured them: they weren't the only animals to start a secret new life. It could be done.

As with anything in life, there is always an element of luck, too. How fortunate that your mother met your father, otherwise they wouldn't have had you! How lucky that you live where you do or you wouldn't be able to find the way home! And what a stroke of luck that you picked up this book – or you wouldn't be reading all about the Bolds right now!

And so it was for the Bolds. Luck was definitely on their side when they landed in England and had to face another tricky passport control situation. Of course the photos in the passports were of the original Fred and Amelia, and looked nothing like Spot and Sue. Dolores had helped them at Kilimanjaro – but what was going to happen now?

Just as they reached the booth and handed their passports to a rather surly, suspicious inspector, a fly landed on his nose. He waved it away but it returned. This happened again and again, until the man sneezed. The sneeze made

PASSPORT CONTROL

NO SMILING !

his eyes all watery, and as he looked from the passports to the Bolds, his vision was rather blurred and the differences – fresh-faced in the photo, hairy in real life; dry-nosed in the photo, wet-nosed in real life; ears on the side of their heads in the photo, sticking up on top of their heads in real life – passed him by. Reaching for his hanky, the inspector waved the Bolds through. They had made it! Now they just had to collect their bags and get to their new home.

(They've often wondered since if this business with the fly was really a coincidence? Perhaps this fly had come with them from the Serengeti, onto the coach, through the airport and onto the plane, maybe hidden in Mrs Bold's handbag. Could it be that this fly knew he might be of vital assistance? We will never know the answer for sure, but I know what I think . . .)

So, to cut a long story medium-length, the Bolds were almost home and dry. Although 'dry' is an unfortunate choice of word, as it happens. When they emerged from the airport it was a very cold November day and pouring with rain. Mr and Mrs Bold had never experienced cold before.

'Brrrrr!' shivered Mr Bold. 'G-g-gosh, it's cold here!'

'Freezation, Fred!' agreed Amelia. Then she noticed the clouds of condensed air as he breathed. 'What's THAT coming out of your mouth?'

'Aagh! And from yours!' said Fred. He looked around. 'It's not just us. Everyone has got great big cloud things coming out of their mouths and noses when they breathe! It's hilarious!' They stood in the taxi queue laughing heartily with every breath, until it was *their* turn to climb into a shiny black cab.

'Where to please, love?' asked the driver.

'41 Fairfield Road, Teddington,' said Mr Bold, remembering the address on the key ring.

'Been somewhere nice?' asked the chatty cab driver, looking at her two passengers in the rear-view mirror.

'Oh, er, we've been on safari!' said Mr Bold.

'Enjoy it?'

'Lovely thanks,' said Mrs Bold.

What do you get if you cross a road with a safari park?

Double yellow lions!

The Bolds had only just arrived in England and didn't know what double yellow lions or lines were, but the punchline sounded funny, so they laughed anyway, which encouraged the taxi driver to tell another joke.

What do you get if you cross an elephant with a bottle of whisky?

Trunk and disorderly!

'Ha ha!' laughed Mr Bold. The more jokes he heard, the better he liked them.

'My name is Jenny, by the way,' said the driver.

'Pleased to meet you, Jenny,' said Mr Bold politely.

Aware that she had a captive, appreciative audience, Jenny continued to chat.

Doing anything nice for Christmas?

I'm having my grandma.

Which will make a change. We normally have turkey!

What's the difference between a wet day and an injured lion?

One pours with rain, the other roars with pain!

Why does a traffic light turn red?

Well, if you had to change in front of everyone, you'd turn red too!

And the jokes continued for the entire journey, until the taxi pulled up outside a lovely semi-detached house in a pleasant suburban road, by which time the Bolds were weak with laughter.

'Here we are, then,' said Jenny. 'You're home.'

Chapter

41 Fairfield Road was a smart house set behind a neat privet hedge. There was a wooden gate with a paved path that led to a front door which was painted a cheerful marigold orange.

Mr and Mrs Bold stood at the gate with their suitcases for a moment, taking it all in.

'Oh my,' said Amelia, her eyes filling with tears of joy. 'Is this really our new home?'

'Yes, dear,' said Fred, eyeing the shrub growing by the front door. 'And what's more, I've got an overwhelming urge to mark my territory by rubbing my bum on that bush.'

'No, Fred,' cautioned Mrs Bold. 'I don't think humans do that sort of thing. At least wait until it's dark.'

'All right. Well let's go inside,' said Fred. 'Have you got the keys?'

Mrs Bold pulled them out of her pocket and jangled them in the air.

Once the door was shut behind them, they put the bags down and began to investigate.

'Ooh! Look!' they cried as they entered each new room. There was so much to see, so much to take in. Hallway, cloakroom, nice big lounge with a comfy pale-blue three-piece suite, ('That'll show the hairs,' tutted Mrs Bold); a dining room with a pine table and six chairs ('Try not to chew the table leg, dear!') and a serving hatch; and a fitted kitchen that led outside to a pretty garden.

'And look in here!' shouted Fred, opening a door from the kitchen into the garage. 'We've got a car!'

'That'll be handy,' said Mrs Bold. 'Once we learn how to drive . . .'

Upstairs were three bedrooms and a bathroom.

It was all a far cry from their den back in Africa, which, although warm and dry, was dark and fuggy and certainly didn't have hot and cold running water, a flushable loo or a garage with a little blue Honda in it.

After they had investigated every room, Mrs Bold stood in the largest bedroom and put her head in her paws for a moment, quite overcome with the sudden change in their surroundings.

Fred came and stood beside her.

'Are you feeling homesick?' he asked, putting his arm round his wife.

'No, Fred,' she said, wiping her eyes. 'I love it here. Why wouldn't I? But I can't help feeling a bit sad. This house, the furniture, the wardrobe full of clothes . . . Can they really be ours?' She glanced around the room and her eyes rested on the bedside cabinet and a framed photo of a happy couple. She picked up the photo.

'Look,' she said. 'This is the original Fred and Amelia. This is their house and their things. What right do we have to be here?'

'May they rest in peace,' said Fred. 'But listen to me. They are gone, remember? It's very sad, and right that we remember them.' He waved his paw around the room. 'But what good is any of this to them now? None at all! I think they'd be glad their home is being put to good use. We will lead a happy life here and I think they'd want that.' He took the photo from Amelia and put it in the bedside drawer.

'Now how about I run us a nice hot pond – or bath, rather? We've had a very long journey, and although I rather like our hyena smell, it might be getting a little pungent, shall we say, for life in Teddington.'

Amelia smiled and gave her husband a kiss on the cheek.

'You're right, Fred,' she said. 'My tail could do with a good soak. It's been cooped up in my bikini briefs for hours!'

'And there's steam coming out of my Y-fronts! Which reminds me . . .

What do you call a leopard that has a bath three times a day?

Spotless!

After their baths – where they learned the hard way that the bottle of shampoo on the shelf wasn't a refreshing fruity drink, and shaking themselves dry as they were used to, instead of using a towel, made a mess up the walls – the two hyenas fell into an exhausted sleep.

It wasn't until they woke up the next morning and were feeling hungry that they discovered there was very little to eat in the house. For breakfast, they made do with some biscuits that they discovered in a cupboard, and Fred managed to open a tin of beans with his teeth. But what were they to do for lunch?

'We'd better go hunting. There must be some zebras round here. Or maybe we can scavenge off a pride of local lions?' Fred suggested.

'Er, no, Fred. There are no lions or zebras here. They live in Africa. And human beings go to things called "shops" for food. I heard someone talking about it on the plane.'

'And where are these "shops", then?' asked Fred, as his tummy rumbled noisily.

'We passed a supermarket on the high street in the taxi yesterday. I could smell all sorts of tasty things,' said Amelia.

'And we don't have to chase it, kill it or fight for it? This is my kinda place!' said a delighted Fred.

'But we do have to pay for it.'

'Pay?'

Mrs Bold delved into her handbag, pulled out her purse and opened it.

'Yes,' she said, producing some ten pound notes. 'This stuff. It's a human thing. It's what the taxi driver asked for yesterday. It's called "money", apparently.

The deal is, someone drives you home or gives you food or whatever and you give them these little bits of paper. I doubt the hot water or the warmth coming from these metal things on the wall are free, either.'

Does money grow on trees?

'No,' said Mrs Bold, shaking her head.

Then why do banks have branches?

Mrs Bold rolled her eyes. 'I can't answer that . . . It's a **strange** business. But ther are quite a few of these bits of paper my handbag, and I've seen some more in a drawer downstairs. The taxi driver also called it "cash".'

Once they'd finished laughing, Mr and Mrs Bold got dressed into some clothes (including hats to cover their ears) from he wardrobes, found a shopping bag and t out for the supermarket. This was the first time they had walked down a street in Teddington or indeed, anywhere else. In Africa, if they met another hyena, they would sniff each other or maybe have a playful wrestle. If they didn't like them they would curl their lips and show their teeth. But it seemed humans didn't do that. Every time the Bolds passed someone in the street they were ignored. Then there was the tricky business of crossing the road: stop signs, green men, honking horns – all were new to the Bolds.

'I'm in quite a tizzy!' said Mrs Bold to her husband.

They wisely decided to watch what everyone else did and copy them.

When they got to the supermarket, the

realised a basket was needed to put their 'prey' in.

'All these delicious smells!' said Mr Bold, his powerful hyena senses overwhelmed with the variety on offer: lamb chops, chicken nuggets, fresh bread, cheese, chocolates. All these were new to the Bolds.

'It's making me a little light-headed!' said Mrs Bold, licking her lips and steadying herself against a shelf.

'Do we just tuck in straight away?' asked Fred.

'No, look. I think we choose what we want then take it over there, where all the beeping noises are coming from. Then we exchange it for cash.'

'It's all so civilised!' said Fred.

'Isn't it!' agreed Amelia. 'No need to catch or snatch.'

So slowly, very slowly, the Bolds got used to living life as humans. Apart from the basic things like food and washing, there was what seemed like a mountain of new things to discover and try to get the hang of.

Imagine never having used a light switch or a television before!

Inevitably mistakes were made. Lots of them: for several days they thought the letter box was where you went to the toilet, they thought curtains were for wiping your bum on, they thought a waste-paper bin was a hat, the hoover was a musical instrument, an umbrella was what you ate your food with, soap was cake and runny honey was shampoo!

They kept their underwear in the fridge, they ate their dinner at the ironing board, cleaned their teeth with yoghurt and ate toothpaste for breakfast. They thought the rotary washing line was for swinging on and the grass mower was for peeling potatoes with. They ate their lunch off saucepan lids, mistook the garden hose for a snake, and assumed that pencils were a tasty snack, forks were hair clips, and that the hedge was where you hung your clothes out to dry.

And, of course, as they slowly learned what things were really for, everything, but everything just continued to make them laugh.

'We've been such silly sausages!' said

Mr Bold. 'I've just watched a cookery programme on that talking box thing—'

'The TV, dear?' interrupted Mrs Bold.

'Yes, that's the one. And guess what?'

'What?'

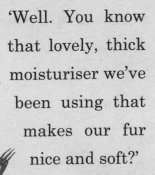

'Well. You know that lovely, thick moisturiser we've been using that makes our fur nice and soft?'

'Yes, dear,' answered Mrs Bold. 'What about it? It rubs in very nicely. And I do so love the smell.'

'Apparently it's not moisturiser at all. It's called butter, and it's what humans spread on bread!'

'No!' said Mrs Bold. 'I can't believe we've been so silly again!' And the Bolds laughed until tears ran down their furry, butter-scented cheeks. Once they'd calmed

down, Mr Bold pointed out that they'd just learned another important lesson.

'Have we, dear?' said Amelia, wiping her face with what she thought was a handkerchief.

'Well, yes. There is an awful lot to learn in this life, but learning can be fun!'

'I'll say!' agreed Mrs Bold, holding out her hanky for inspection. 'I've just learned this handkerchief thing is in fact a pair of knickers!'

And of course they both collapsed with laughter once more.

Chapter

However, despite all the laughter, there was something more serious that they soon learned about.

Nearly every morning, brown papery things kept on arriving in the letter box. They naively assumed that these were leaves blown through by a gust of wind, but they actually turned out to be things called 'bills' that required paying with that other papery stuff known as 'money'. And the money they had found in the house was running out.

'Well what happens if we don't pay these silly bill-things?' asked Mrs Bold, after looking in her purse and finding it empty.

'Nothing much,' said Mr Bold cheerfully. 'We saw that programme about it on the telly-box thing. For some reason they send some babies round. I can't think why.'

'Babies?' questioned Mrs Bold.

'So they said.'

Mrs Bold looked thoughtful for a moment. 'Oh no, you've got it wrong, Fred, I remember now, it was bailiffs, not babies, silly.'

'What's a bailiff?'

'A debt collector. Much less pleasant than a baby, I think you'll find. If you can't pay your bills, the bailiffs come round and take items of value away from your home.'

'Yikes!' said Fred.

'We'd better get hold of some more money, quick, I think,' said Mrs Bold soberly.

Where does a fish keep his money?

In a river bank!

'Stop it, Fred, this is serious!' said Mrs Bold, trying not to laugh.

Laughing made the Bolds feel better, but it didn't really help matters.

After some investigation, Mrs Bold

came up with a solution one morning. 'It seems that humans go to work. They have things called jobs. They get paid with money and then they can pay their bills and buy food, clothes and everything else.'

'Really?' said Fred. 'I wondered why everyone seems to rush about every morning as if they're in a hurry.'

'They're on their way to work,' pointed out Mrs Bold.

'So how do we get one of these jobs? Can we buy one?'

'No, don't be silly,' said Mrs Bold. 'I've seen some advertised in the back of the *Teddington Gazette*. Let's have a look . . . Job Vacancies.'

There were lots of jobs Mr and Mrs Bold fancied doing.

'Dental Receptionist! We've got lovely teeth, haven't we?' said Mr Bold enthusiastically.

'Yes, dear, we have. But I don't think we'd want to boast about them, do you?'

'Ah, no, you're right. Might give us away, eh?'

'Agreed. Retail Assistant?'

'Oh yes! We know all about tails, we could do that! "How may I assist you with your tail, sir? Needs a good brush, does it? Leave it to me, sir!" When can we start?'

'No, Fred. It says it means working in a shop. Retail means selling things. And it's a posh clothes shop.' She looked her husband up and down. 'I don't think we'd be right for that, somehow. We've only just got the hang of clothes ourselves.' She returned to the list. 'Waiting staff?'

'Yup.' Fred nodded. 'I can wait. Did it for hours waiting for prey in the wild. Watch!' He stood motionless for several seconds. 'See. I'm waiting patiently. Waiting, waiting, waiting. Why anyone would want to pay me for waiting around,

I can't imagine. But I'm very good at it.'

Mrs Bold shook her head. 'Waiting means waiting on tables in a restaurant. You can't do that. You'd be a dreadful waiter. You'd lick the plates. And so would I, to be honest. Couldn't resist!'

There were lots of jobs on offer, but nothing the Bolds could seriously imagine themselves doing.

'I've realised that the trick with jobs,' said Mr Bold when they were almost at the end of the list, 'is to do something you're good at. So what am I good at?'

'Er,' said Mrs Bold. 'Well, er, let me think . . .'

'There must be something!'

'Well, back in Africa you were very good at chasing and catching antelope.'

'There we have it!' said Mr Bold, jumping to his feet. 'Aren't there any jobs like that? Is there a professional antelope chaser required?'

Mrs Bold shook her head. 'No, Fred. Nothing like that at all, I'm afraid. Not in Teddington.'

'I'm good at scratching fleas! Any flea scratchers needed?'

Mrs Bold checked the list again. 'Nope. I'm afraid not.'

They both stared gloomily at the newspaper, wondering what they could do.

Chapter

Sadly, it didn't seem as if there were any jobs suitable for the Bolds and their particular talents. A few days later, they had no money left at all. They ate all the food they found in tins at the back of the cupboard. They chomped their way through a leather handbag, some gloves and a belt, but they weren't very tasty or nutritious. Eventually they were driven back to their old hyena ways – hunting and scavenging.

Mrs Bold went creeping out under the cover of darkness wearing a large hat (well, she thought it was a hat, but you and I would recognise it as a lampshade) and caught a few squirrels and a pigeon. Mr Bold rummaged in next door's bins when no one was looking and found a half-eaten apple pie and some potato peelings.

Of course Mr and Mrs Bold didn't mind getting food this way – it was what they were used to after all. But there was a risk that they would be spotted. On her

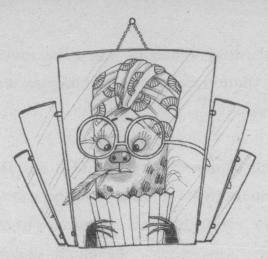

way home from a hunt one evening, Mrs Bold wondered why people were staring at her more often than usual and it wasn't until she looked in the hall mirror that she discovered she had a telltale grey feather sticking out of her mouth. And the neighbours heard their bin lids clanking one night and came outside with a torch: Mr Bold had to hide inside the bin for half an hour until the coast was clear. Their nocturnal activities were becoming dangerous – if they were caught then their true hyena identities would be revealed and their new life in Teddington would be over.

But it wasn't only f°°d that the Bolds needed money for. There were bills for gas, water, electricity and all manner of other household expenses that kept arriving – some of them now printed in red, which apparently means they are urgent and must be paid without delay, or else.

'If the babies – I mean bailiffs – arrive, what shall we do?' asked a worried Mrs Bold.

'We could growl at them,' offered

Mr Bold. 'Or nip them on the ankle if necessary?'

'I don't think that will help in the long run,' said Mrs Bold. 'It won't make the bills go away, and they'd probably call the police.'

Mr Bold's face lit up.

What did the policeman say to his tummy?

You are under a vest!

Mrs Bold cackled with delight at Mr Bold's joke.

'Oh Fred, you are funny! That's one thing you *are* good at.'

'I wish I could get a job just being funny,' said Mr Bold, wistfully.

Now, wishes are powerful things in my experience. Have you ever made a wish and then had it come true? Like wishing you could have chips for tea? Or wishing the rain would stop so you can go outside to play? Or wishing you could have a baby brother or sister? It's as if someone is listening to our wishes and then grants them. No one can explain this. But be careful what you wish for, because sometimes – really quite often – wishes do come true! That is exactly what happened to the Bolds . . .

It was a week later and things were getting desperate. The Bolds had eaten most of the plants in the garden and even pinched the scraps of stale bread from next door's bird table. They were contemplating chewing the chair legs to try and stop the pangs of hunger, when there was a rattle of the letterbox and a thud on the doormat.

'Ah, the *Gazette* is here!' said Mrs Bold, racing to get the paper.

'Can we eat it?' asked Mr Bold. 'Might be nice with marmalade.'

'Not yet. Let's see if there are any jobs on offer first,' said Mrs Bold. And what a good thing it was that they didn't eat it! There, at the top of the 'Job Vacancies' page, was the perfect job for Mr Bold.

'FRED!' cried Mrs Bold. 'Listen to this! "Joke Writer wanted urgently for Teddington Christmas Cracker Factory. No qualifications needed, but successful applicant must be extremely funny."'

'This is the job I've been waiting for!' said Fred excitedly. The job he'd wished for, he might have added. Fred called the number in the paper at once and arranged an interview for the next day.

He wore a smart tweed jacket and a red tie he'd found in the wardrobe. A trilby hat covered his ears nicely. He even had a squirt of aftershave – which was really wasp killer, but it smelled lovely, according to Mrs Bold.

The Christmas Cracker Factory was a twenty-minute walk from Fairfield Road and Mr Bold arrived early for his interview, so the receptionist kindly made him a cup of tea.

'Help yourself to biscuits,' she said, placing a large plate

piled high with custard creams in front of
him. Mr Bold's eyes lit up. All he'd had
for breakfast was a few snails he'd found
in the garden and some birdseed. So help
himself he did. He thoughtfully put a few
in his pocket for Mrs Bold, then scoffed the
rest. He was therefore in a very jolly mood
when he was called into the main office
to be interviewed by the factory owner, a
friendly, sparkly-eyed woman called Mrs
Greenwood. After some pleasant chitchat
about the weather, the real test began.

'We need our joke writer to have a wide
range of funny jokes up his or her sleeve.
Jokes of all sorts. So I'll say a subject and
you tell me a joke. Ready, Mr Bold?'

'Ready when you are!' said Fred,
clearing his throat and dusting some

biscuit crumbs off his tie.

'Let's start with . . . volcano?'

What did the volcano say to the other volcano?

I lava you!

'Excellent! Elephant?'

What time is it when the elephant sits on the fence?

Time to fix the fence!

'Ha ha! Ducks?'

What time do ducks wake up?

The quack of dawn!

'Great! Dinosaurs?'

What do you call a dinosaur with no eyes?

Doyouthinkhesaurus?!

'Brilliant! School teachers?'

What do you do if a teacher rolls her eyes at you?

Roll them back!

'Excellent!' exclaimed Mrs Greenwood. 'You're **very** good at this, Mr Bold. Let's try some more. Ghosts?'

Why are ghosts such bad liars?

Because you can see right through them!

'Good one! Bees?'

Why do bees have sticky hair?

Because they use honeycombs!

'Another corker. Vampires?'

What do you get if you cross a vampire with a snowman?

Frostbite!

'This is all very impressive,' said Mrs Greenwood, making a few notes on her pad and chuckling to herself. 'Now let's see how you are with riddles. Know any good ones?'

'Oh, yes,' said Mr Bold confidently. 'Try these . . .

What starts with P and ends in E and has a million letters in it?

Post office!

What has a face and two hands but no arms or legs?

A clock!

What can you catch but can't throw?

A cold!

Mrs Greenwood held up her hand. 'OK, Mr Bold! I see you know lots of riddles. Last category is knock-knock jokes.'

Without a pause Mr Bold began.

'Oh, Mr Bold, how on **earth** did you get to be so funny?' laughed Mrs Greenwood.

'It comes very naturally,' replied Fred modestly.

A few days later a phone call informed Fred Bold he was appointed to the job of Joke Writer at the Christmas Cracker Factory. He and Mrs Bold celebrated with steak and chips.

And as is often the way, once their luck changed, things just got better and better. To cover her ears, Mrs Bold always wore hats – or what she thought were hats. Before leaving the house she often grabbed whatever she could find. Cushions, wastepaper bins, shopping baskets, a birdcage – as long as her head and ears weren't on view, she was happy. Then, when she was out and about, she started to get admiring looks and compliments from other women about her eye-catching headwear.

'Where did you get that lovely and most unusual hat from?' asked a woman on the bus one day.

'Oh,' said Mrs Bold, glancing up at the flowerpot she had slung on to her head that morning and then, because it was a bit wobbly, secured with a tartan tea towel tied under her chin, 'I, um, made it!'

'Did you?' gasped the woman. 'Do you think you could make me one? Only I'm going to a wedding next week and a hat like that would be just the thing.'

'Er, certainly,' said Mrs Bold.

'I'll pay you, of course,' said the woman. And so Mrs Bold's hat business began. The woman on the bus told her friend, who also wanted a hat, and she told her friends and so on and so on. The whole thing mushroomed. Within a few weeks Mrs Bold opened a stall at Teddington market, selling hats of every description. During the week she made hats out of whatever she could find – the crazier the better, it seemed, as far as her customers were concerned: old shoes, empty tins, dustbin lids, birds' nests, even cardboard

food wrappings. Then on Saturdays she sold them at the stall. The more bizarre the hats, the more her customers snapped them up.

So with Mr Bold's wages from the Cracker Factory and the income Mrs Bold's hats generated, the Bolds could pay all their bills and afford to go shopping for as much food as they wanted.

They were very happy and contented. They didn't think they could be any happier – but they were wrong about that . . .

One evening they decided to treat themselves to dinner at the local burger bar and that evening Mrs Bold had a tummy ache. But it wasn't a dodgy burger, as she at first believed – in fact she was having a baby. Then another. Or perhaps we should say pups!

Yes, that was the night the twins Betty and Bobby were born.

The moment they arrived, Mr Bold looked at them and wondered if it was too soon to tell them a joke. He decided it wasn't.

What did the mummy snake say to the crying baby snake?

"Stop crying and viper your nose!"

Chapter

'So that is our family secret,' Mr Bold concluded to his children, who were wide awake still, fascinated and amazed by everything they had heard. Well, you would be, wouldn't you? Imagine if you'd just found out you were really a hyena living a secret life.

'And that is why we Bolds have tails,' added Mrs Bold.

'And why we're hairy, with pointy ears,' added Mr Bold.

'And why we laugh so much!' chortled Mrs Bold.

'We thought you should know all of this before you start school tomorrow.'

Bobby and Betty looked at each other and giggled.

'Wowsers!' said Betty.

'We are special!' said Bobby.

'Yes, you are,' said their mother. 'Very special. And you always will be. Now settle down.' And she tucked them up.

'So,' said Betty, rubbing her eyes. 'We are hyenas, but no one must ever find out?'

'Correct,' said Mr and Mrs Bold as one.

'And we mustn't draw attention to ourselves,' said Bobby, snuggling under his duvet and yawning – it was getting rather late.

'Learning can be fun!'

'Dreams really can come true!'

'And everything will always . . . be . . . all right in the end,' said Betty slowly. By the time she had finished speaking, both twins' eyes had closed and a few seconds later they were fast asleep.

Mrs Bold turned the bedside light out and Mr Bold gave both pups a **gentle** stroke of their ears. Then they crept out of the bedroom and went downstairs to prepare the twins' packed lunches for their very first day at school.

'I think that went **rather** well,' said Mrs Bold as she cut four thick slices of bread.

Then the two hyenas laughed so much, they each had to cover their snouts with a tea towel in case they woke the twins.

THE END

More Bold Adventures!

If you've enjoyed this story, then why not read more of the Bolds' adventures! Will their secret be discovered? Will the twins be able to hide their tails during P.E. lessons? And will the family always be able to see the funny side of things?

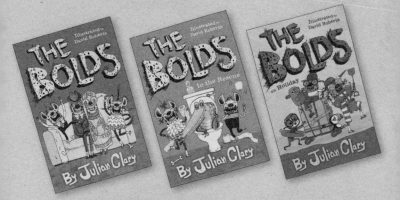

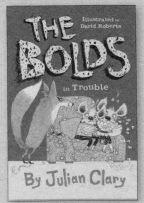

Book 4 Coming Soon!

MR BOLD'S JOKES

Why did the bus stop?
Because it saw the zebra crossing!

What do you get if you cross a road with a safari park?
Double yellow lions!

What do you call a pig who steals things?
A hamburglar!

What do you get if you cross an elephant with a bottle of whisky?
Trunk and disorderly!

Doing anything nice for Christmas?
I'm having my grandma. Which will make a change. We normally have turkey!

What do you give a sick hog?
Oinkment!

What's the difference between a wet day and an injured lion?
One pours with rain, the other roars with pain!

Why does a traffic light turn red?
Well, if you had to change in front of everyone, you'd turn red too!

Knock, Knock!
Who's there?
Cash!
Cash who?
Cash me if you can!

Where does a fish keep his money?
In a river bank!

What time do ducks wake up?
The quack of dawn!

What do you call a leopard that has a bath three times a day?
Spotless!

Knock, Knock!
Who's there?
Cash!
Cash who?
I knew you were a nut!

Does money grow on trees?
No.
Then why do banks have branches?

What did the policeman say to his tummy?
You are under a vest!

What did the volcano say to the other volcano?
I lava you!

What time is it when the elephant sits on the fence?
Time to fix the fence!

What do you call a dinosaur with no eyes?
Doyouthinkhesaurus?!

What do you do if a teacher rolls her eyes at you?
Roll them back!

Why are ghosts such bad liars?
Because you can see right through them!

Why do bees have sticky hair?
Because they use honeycombs!

What do you get if you cross a vampire with a snowman?
Frostbite!

What starts with P and ends in E and has a million letters in it?
Post office!

What has a face and two hands but no arms or legs?
A clock!

What can you catch but not throw?
A cold!

Knock, knock!
Who's there?
Mikey.
Mikey who?
Mikey doesn't fit in the lock!

Knock, knock!
Who's there?
Howard.
Howard who?
Howard I know?

Knock, knock!
Who's there?
Frank.
Frank who?
Frank you for being my friend!

What did the mummy snake say to the crying baby snake?
'Stop crying and viper your nose!'

Knock, knock!
Who's there?
Loaf!
Loaf who?
I don't just like bread, I loaf it!

These animals are also in disguise. Can you unscramble the letters to reveal the real creature?

KANSE

FRIGAFE

LIDOCORCE

OPENTALE

OLNI

DID YOU ENJOY READING ABOUT THE BOLDS?

Here's another rib-tickling story you might also enjoy!

Take a peek at the first chapter of . . .

Spangles McNasty
and the Fish of Gold

BITTERLYBAY

Steve Webb
ILLUSTRATED BY CHRIS MOULD

First published in 2016 by
Andersen Press Limited
20 Vauxhall Bridge Road
London SW1V 2SA
www.andersenpress.co.uk

British Library Cataloguing in Publication Data available.

ISBN 978 1 78344 400 7

The Spangler

Spangles McNasty was nasty to everyone and everything, everywhere, all of the time.

He had a heart as cold as a box of fish fingers in a supermarket freezer, a brain brimming with badness and a head bristling with baldness.

There was only one thing Spangles liked more than being nasty, and that was collecting spangly things: shiny, sparkly, glittery, spangly things.

Of course, when he said 'collecting', he meant 'taking without asking or paying', or as everyone else calls it, stealing.

A perfect day for Spangles McNasty would start with a handful of his favourite breakfast – cold, greasy chips, scooped from a bin on the seafront so he didn't have to pay for them. He'd follow this with pulling faces at old ladies, shouting at babies and, if at all possible, farting in the local library. But, best of all, it would end with collecting something spangly on the way home.

If he could collect something spangly from an old lady with a baby in a library, whilst eating cold chips, farting, pulling a face and shouting all at the same time, it would quite possibly be the happiest day of his entire nasty life.

Sadly for Spangles, that day had so far escaped him, but each and every morning he awoke with a new nasty hope in his frozen-fish-finger-box heart. 'Maybe today's the day, Trevor,' he would say hopefully.

Trevor was a goldfish. He lived with Spangles in a rusty old camper van, which had ended a long adventure-filled travelling life at a scrap yard, where it would have been recycled, had it not been for Spangles McNasty walking in one afternoon and 'collecting' it while no one was looking.

He had been doing his nasty collecting business in it ever since.

Camper vans are, of course, little completely mobile homes (like tortoises, but faster and with more seat belts). However, Spangles' camper rarely left his home town of Bitterly Bay, except when he was away on special collecting business. Nestled in a curve of coastline between the Jelly Cliffs in the north and Sandylands to the south, Bitterly

Bay was 'home spangly home' to Spangles McNasty. An expression he liked so much, he'd written it with his finger in the dirt that covered his van, just above where he'd written, 'Trevor is a stinker'.

Trevor swam in tiny contented circles round and round a small glass bowl hanging from the camper's rear-view mirror, where most people hang air fresheners shaped like Christmas trees.

Spangles kept Trevor hanging in the window of his camper van for two reasons. Firstly, so he had someone to talk to, and secondly, to watch the sunshine spangle on his shiny golden skin, which it was doing magnificently on the sunny Saturday morning our story begins.

Trevor swam on peacefully in his fish-bowl camper-van home, parked outside a newsagent's. He was as happy as a fish, as the old saying goes (well, it doesn't, but it should). Spangles, meanwhile, was inside the newsagent's,  buying the local newspaper. He too, was as happy as a fish.

Trevor stopped swimming momentarily and watched the familiar baldy figure of Spangles approach.

Spangles strode purposefully through the newsagent's, swinging his patched-up pinstripe-suited arms and legs almost high enough to flick his threadbare baseball boots at the ceiling.

He whistled merrily at his naughty reflection in the glass door as he was leaving, wriggling his

large handlebar moustache and allowing his bushy caterpillar eyebrows a quick dance before trying to slam the shop door behind him. Rather annoyingly, it had one of those self-closing-smoothly mechanisms. Muttering something nasty under his breath, Spangles climbed back into the driver's seat of his camper and slammed that door instead. The van shook, setting off its ancient alarm, which wailed like an unhappy elephant at Weight Watchers. He then leant on the horn accidentally-on-purpose just to be sure.

The sunshine, the newsagent, the milkman,

Trevor and Spangles were all awake, but the rest of the world was still tucked up in bed, sound asleep. Well, they had been.

'**Wakey, wakey**,' Spangles said brightly, unfolding his newspaper, before turning to Trevor. 'Hello there, my spangly friend,' he beamed. 'And may I say how super-shiny you is lookin' this **beautiful sunny mornin**'!' Spangles was feeling unusually cheerful, and it wasn't just because he'd woken 146 local residents somewhat earlier than they'd like on a Saturday. He had nasty plans for the day ahead, and nothing made him happier than carefully prepared nastiness.

'Imagine when you're fully growed!' Spangles said, grinning manically at the shiny fish. He believed completely that goldfish grow to the size

of whales, and are, in fact, made of solid gold. 'Imagine the spangles on that, Trev!' he said, but Trevor wasn't listening, he was busy swimming in and out of his little castle, playing soldiers.

'Have you seen today's headline in the paper?' Spangles held up the front page of the **Bitterly Daily Blah Blah** for Trevor to read. Trevor said nothing. He couldn't read.

'Says here, "More goldfish thefts! Sandylands is the third seaside town to be hit by the **mysterious goldfish thief**."' Spangles chuckled to himself. 'How very strange, eh, Trev. Some people are right peculiar, ain't they? What kind of a nut box would collect shiny golden fish?'

He waited a polite second or two for Trevor's response and then shouted over his shoulder to the living area, 'All right in the back?'

There was no reply.

There was no reply because there was no one living in the living area. No one apart from 326 goldfish, and they never spoke. This was something that did not especially worry Spangles. As long as they all grew as big as whales and made him rich, he'd be happy.

As Spangles turned the key in the ignition, the engine grumbled its annoyance at being started so early in the morning. The bright sunshine streamed through the front window and shimmered on Trevor's shiny golden fins.

'Ah, Trev, me old spangler,' Spangles said, as the camper lurched down the road, coughing thick clouds of unspeakable filth from its rusty exhaust. 'This is going to be a right super spangler of a day, I can just feel it. Bitterly Bay, here we come.'

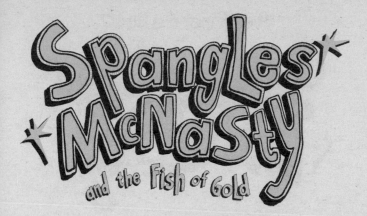

Spangles McNasty and the Fish of Gold

Steve Webb
Illustrated by Chris Mould

Spangles McNasty is convinced that he can get rich quick by stealing goldfish – after all, aren't they made of solid gold? Together with his friend Sausage-face Pete, he decides to find the great Fish of Gold. Only young Freddie Taylor can stop Spangles' dastardly plan, in a tale full of time-travelling jet skis, madcap chases and haunted custard.

'Unadulterated fun!'
Lovereading

'Ludicrous and funny'
BookTrust

Read more about

Steve Webb
Illustrated by Chris Mould

Spangles McNasty has inherited a rickety old rollercoaster called the Tunnel of Doom. If he wants to make any lovely money from it, he and his best friend Sausage-face Pete will need to do some hard work and repair it. Spangles won't stand for that, so he comes up with a dastardly plot to get rich quick. It's up to local boy Freddie Taylor to stop him in his tracks!

978 1 78344 508 0

When the legendarily famous and very sparkly Diamond Skull pirate hat comes to Bitterly Bay Museum, Spangles and his best mate Sausage-face Pete want to get their thieving fingers on it. But they haven't reckoned on local boy and all-round good egg Freddie Taylor and his cunning plan to mix things up with a clever hat trick . . .

978 1 78344 638 4

WORLD
BOOK
DAY

Hello

We hope you enjoyed this book.

Proudly brought to you by **WORLD BOOK DAY**,

the **BIGGEST CELEBRATION** of the **magic** and **fun** of **storytelling**.

We are the **bringer of books to readers** everywhere

and a **charity** on a **MISSION**

to take you on a **READING JOURNEY**.

EXPLORE
new worlds
(and bookshops!)

EXPAND
your
imagination

DISCOVER
some of the very
best authors and
illustrators with us.

A **LOVE OF READING** is one of life's greatest gifts.

And this book is **OUR** gift to **YOU**.

HAPPY READING.
HAPPY WORLD BOOK DAY!

WORLD BOOK DAY

SHARE A STORY

Discover and share stories from breakfast to bedtime.

THREE ways to continue **YOUR** reading adventure

1 VISIT YOUR LOCAL BOOKSHOP

Your go-to destination for awesome reading recommendations and events with your favourite authors and illustrators.

FIND YOUR LOCAL BOOKSHOP
booksellers.org.uk/ bookshopsearch

2 JOIN YOUR LOCAL LIBRARY

Browse and borrow from a huge selection of books, get expert ideas of what to read next and take part in wonderful family reading activities – all for FREE!

FIND YOUR LOCAL LIBRARY
findmylibrary.co.uk

3 GO ONLINE AT WORLDBOOKDAY.COM

Fun podcasts, activities, games, videos, downloads, competitions, new books galore and all the latest book news.

Illustrations © Jim Field

SPONSORED BY

NATIONAL BOOK tokens

Celebrate stories. Love reading.